# The Call of the Wild

### Jack London

Condensed and Adapted by
KATHRYN R. KNIGHT

Illustrated by
MICHEAL FISHER

Cover Illustrated by
DOM D'ANDREA

bendon

The Bendon Junior Classics have been
adapted and illustrated with care and thought
to introduce you to a world of famous authors, characters, ideas,
and great stories that have been loved for generations.

Editor — Kathryn Knight
Creative Director — Gina Rhodes Haynes
And the entire classics project team

THE CALL OF THE WILD

Copyright © 2017 Bendon, Inc.
Ashland, Ohio 44805 • 1-888-5-BENDON
bendonpub.com

Printed in the United States of America

A *note to the reader*—

A classic story rests in your hands. The characters are famous. The tale is timeless.

This Junior Classic edition of *The Call of the Wild* has been carefully condensed and adapted from the original version (which you really *must* read when you're ready for every detail). We kept the well-known phrases for you. We kept Jack London's style. And we kept the important imagery and heart of the tale.

Literature is terrific fun! It encourages you to think. It helps you dream. It is full of heroes and villains, suspense and humor, adventure and wonder, and new ideas. It introduces you to writers who reach out across time to say: "Do you want to hear a story I wrote?"

Curl up and enjoy.

# CONTENTS

BUCK — a large St. Bernard/Scotch shepherd dog stolen from Judge Miller's estate in California

JUDGE MILLER — Buck's first owner

MANUEL — Judge Miller's hired gardener's helper who kidnaps and sells Buck

THE MAN IN THE RED SWEATER — the dog-trader who "breaks" Buck

PERRAULT AND FRANÇOIS — French Canadian dog-sledders who work for the Canadian Government, Buck's first owners in the Klondike

Dog team of Perrault and François:

CURLY — a Newfoundland dog bought at the same time as Buck

SPITZ — a crafty white dog from Spitzbergen who leads the team

DAVE — a quiet dog who holds the wheeler position next to the sled

BILLEE — a friendly husky dog, Joe's brother

JOE — a mean husky dog, brother of Billee

SOL-LEKS — a one-eyed dog whose name means "Angry One"

PIKE, DUB AND DOLLY — three dogs added during the trek

TEEK AND KOONA — native huskies added at Rink Rapids

THE SCOTCH HALF-BREED — the mail carrier, Buck's second owner in the Klondike

CHARLES — an American tenderfoot in search of adventure, Buck's third owner in the Klondike

MERCEDES — Charles's wife

HAL — Mercedes's brother, the driver of the team

JOHN THORNTON — prospector in the Klondike who rescues Buck

NIGHT AND SKEET — John Thornton's dogs

HANS AND PETE —John Thornton's partners

"BLACK" BURTON — a bully in Dawson, Yukon

MATTHEWSON — a bragging man who makes a bet with Thornton

THE WILD BROTHER — a wild wolf who befriends Buck

THE YEEHATS — a native Indian tribe of the Yukon Territory

# The Call
## of the Wild

# CHAPTER ONE

# A Kidnapped King

Buck did not read the newspapers, or he would have known that trouble was ahead. Trouble not just for him but for every strong dog with warm, long hair along the western coastline. Men had found gold in the Arctic, and these men wanted dogs. The dogs they wanted were heavy dogs with strong muscles to pull dog sleds and with furry coats to protect them from the frost.

Buck lived at a big house in the sunny Santa Clara Valley. Judge Miller's place, it was called. It was a large, beautiful home with wrap-around porches and a long driveway. The estate had wide lawns with great stables, grape arbors, green pastures, orchards, and berry patches. Then there was the big cement tank where Judge Miller's boys took their morning swim and kept cool in the hot afternoon.

Buck ruled over this great estate. Here he was born, and here he had lived the four years of his life. There were other dogs, but they did not count. The house dogs and the kennel dogs came and went. But Buck was neither house dog nor kennel dog. The whole place was his. He jumped into the swimming tank, and went hunting with the Judge's sons. He went with Mollie and Alice, the Judge's daughters, on long walks. On wintry nights he lay at the Judge's feet before the roaring library fire. He carried the Judge's grandsons on his back, or rolled them in the grass, and played with them in the orchards. Buck was king—king over all the other dogs and every person at the Miller estate.

His father, Elmo, had been a huge St. Bernard, the Judge's favorite. Buck was not so large—he weighed only one hundred and forty pounds—for his mother, Shep, had been a Scotch shepherd dog. Nevertheless, he carried himself like a much larger dog, like the king he was, with great pride.

And this was the life Buck led in the fall of 1897, when the Klondike gold dragged men from all over the world into the frozen North. But Buck did not read the newspapers. He did not know that men's hearts could be turned with greed. Manuel, one of the gardener's helpers, *was* such a man whose heart had turned, and his greedy eyes had fallen on Buck—*a perfect sled dog.*

The Judge was at a meeting and the boys were at a club on the sad night of Manuel's crime. No one saw him take Buck and lead him through the orchard for an evening "stroll." And only one man saw them arrive at the little train station known as College Park. This one man talked with Manuel and handed him money.

"Are you going to tie him up?" the stranger asked gruffly.

Manuel doubled a piece of stout rope around Buck's neck under the collar. "Twist it, and you'll choke him plenty," said Manuel.

Buck did not resist the rope. He had learned to trust men he knew. But when the ends of the rope were placed in the stranger's hands, he growled to make the man let go. To his surprise, the rope tightened around his neck, shutting off his breath.

In a quick rage he sprang at the man, but the man was ready. He threw Buck onto his back and tightened the rope more. Never in all his life had Buck been so cruelly treated, and never in all his life had he been so angry. But his strength left him, his eyes closed, and he fainted from the rope and the pain. He was not even aware when the train came and the two men threw him into the baggage car.

The next he knew, he was being jolted along in something moving, and his tongue was hurting. The shriek of a train whistle told him where he was. He was kidnapped! He was a kidnapped king now full of anger. He opened his eyes and saw a man in the baggage car. The man's hand sprang to pull the rope, but Buck was too quick for him. His jaws closed on the hand—and he held on even as he was choked once again.

Later, in a small saloon, the man complained of his night's ride. "All I get is fifty dollars for this here dog," he grumbled, "and I wouldn't do it over for a *thousand* dollars!"

He held Buck firmly by the rope. The man's hand was wrapped up, and his pants were ripped from knee to ankle.

"How much did the other guy get?" the saloon-keeper asked.

"A hundred—wouldn't take a penny less."

"That makes a hundred and fifty dollars," the saloon-keeper said, "and he's worth it, or I don't know dogs. Here, lend me a hand with this brass collar he's wearing."

Dazed and in pain, Buck once more was thrown down and choked. The two men held him down as they filed his heavy brass collar from off his neck. Then the rope was removed, and he was flung into a cage-like crate. Without his collar, no one would ever know that he was the king of Judge Miller's estate.

There he lay for the rest of the night. He could not understand what it all meant. What did they want with him, these strange men? Why were they keeping him in this narrow crate? Several times during the night he sprang to his feet when the shed door rattled open, expecting to see the Judge, or the boys at least. But each time it was the ugly face of the saloon-keeper that looked in on him. And each time his hope turned into a savage growl.

In the morning, four men entered and picked up the crate—evil-looking men. Buck stormed and raged at them through the bars. They only laughed and poked sticks at him as the crate was lifted into a wagon. Then Buck began a long journey—on a wagon, a truck, a ferry steamer, and finally on yet another train—passing through many hands to a place he knew not where.

# CHAPTER TWO

# The Law of Club

For two days and nights Buck neither ate nor drank. Shaking, he flung himself against the bars. The hunger was painful, but the thirst for water was torture. His throat was dry, his tongue was swollen, and his body burned with fever.

He was glad for one thing—the rope was off his neck. Never again would a man get a rope around his neck. For in those two days and nights of torment, he was changed into a new animal— a raging beast. He was so changed that the Judge himself would not have recognized him. The train workers were glad to see this fierce beast leave the train at Seattle.

Four men carefully carried the crate from the wagon into a small yard. A stout man with a red sweater came out and signed the book for the driver. Buck knew this was the next tormentor and he hurled himself against the bars. The man smiled grimly, and brought out a hatchet and a club.

"You ain't going to take him out *now?*" the driver asked.

"Sure," the man replied, prying the crate open with the hatchet.

The four men, who had carried the crate in, quickly scattered and got atop a safe, high wall to watch.

Buck snarled, growled, and rushed at the sides of the crate.

"Now, you red-eyed devil," said the man in the red sweater, when the crate was dashed open. He dropped the hatchet and shifted the club to his right hand.

And Buck truly *was* a red-eyed devil—with hair bristling, mouth foaming, a mad glitter in his bloodshot eyes. Straight at the man he launched his one hundred and forty pounds of fury. In midair, just as his jaws were about to close on the man,

he received a shocking blow. He whirled over, hitting the ground on his back and side. He had never been struck by a club in his life and did not understand. With a snarl that was part bark and more scream, he was again on his feet and he launched into the air. And again the shock came and he was brought crushingly to the ground. This time he knew it was the club, but a dozen times he charged, and a dozen times the club broke the charge and smashed him down.

Buck crawled to his feet, too dazed to rush. He staggered limply about, the blood flowing from nose and mouth and ears. Then the man gave him a frightful blow on the nose. All the pain he had ever known was nothing compared with this. With a lion-like roar, he again hurled himself at the man. The man struck a final blow and Buck crumpled up and went down, knocked completely senseless.

"He can break a dog, that's what I say," one of the men on the wall exclaimed.

"I'd rather break wild mustangs any day," was the reply of the driver, as he climbed on the wagon and started the horses.

Buck's senses came back to him, but not his strength. He lay where he had fallen, and from there he watched the man in the red sweater.

The man read over the note that came with the crate.

"Well, Buck, my boy," he went on in a friendly voice, "we've had our little lesson, and the best thing we can do is to let it go at that. You've learned your place, and I know mine. Be a good dog and all will go well. Be a bad dog, and I'll beat the stuffing outa you. Understand?"

As he spoke he patted the head he had so cruelly pounded with no mercy. Buck's hair bristled at the touch of the hand, but he lay still. When the man brought him water, he drank eagerly, and later gulped down a meal of raw meat, chunk by chunk, from the man's hand.

He was beaten (he knew that), but he was not broken. He saw that he stood no chance against a man with a club. He had learned the lesson, and he would never forget it.

As the days went by, other dogs came, in crates and at the ends of ropes. Some came quietly, and some raged and roared.

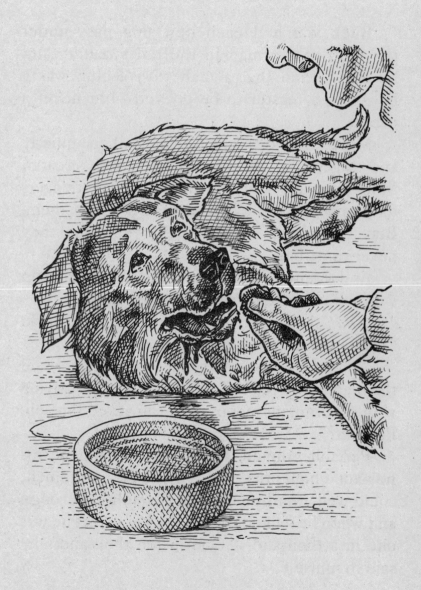

Buck watched each new dog pass under the club of the man in the red sweater. And he knew then that a man with a club was a lawgiver, a master to be obeyed—but never a friend.

More strangers came who talked quietly and eagerly to the man in the red sweater. Money passed between them and the strangers took one or more of the dogs away with them. Buck wondered where they went, for they never came back.

And then *his* time came. A little wrinkled man who spoke broken English spotted Buck.

"*Ola!*" he cried, when his eyes lit upon Buck. "Dat one bully dog! Eh? How much?"

"Three hundred, and that is a bargain," said the man in the red sweater. "And you are paying with government money. You can afford that, eh, Perrault?"

Perrault grinned. For so fine an animal this was not a high price. The Canadian Government could well afford such a dog. Perrault knew dogs, and when he looked at Buck he knew that he was one in a thousand—"One in ten thousand," he said to himself.

Buck saw money pass between them. Perrault also bought another dog—a good-natured Newfoundland named Curly—and he led the two dogs away. That was the last Buck saw of the man in the red sweater.

As Curly and he looked at the shoreline from the deck of the boat, it was the last he saw of the warm land of the Southland coast.

# CHAPTER THREE

# The Law of Fang

Curly and Buck were taken below deck by Perrault and handed over to a large man called François. Both men were French Canadian, tan and weathered from Klondike life. This was a new kind of man to Buck. He did not befriend them, but he grew to respect them. He soon learned that Perrault and François were fair men, but too wise in the way of dogs to be fooled by dogs.

Between decks, Buck and Curly joined two other dogs. One was a big, snow-white fellow from Spitzbergen who had been brought away by a whaling captain. He was friendly—but not to be trusted. "Spitz," as he was called, would smile

while he planned some sneaky trick—and he indeed proved himself to be sneaky. When he stole from Buck's food at the first meal, Buck sprang to punish him. Just then the lash of François's whip sang through the air, reaching the white dog first. Buck observed that this at least was fair treatment from this man with the whip.

The other dog was called "Dave." He was a quiet fellow who wanted to be left alone. His eyes told the others that there would be trouble if he were bothered. When the boat rolled and pitched, Buck and Curly became half-wild with fear. But Dave merely raised his head as though annoyed, glanced their way, yawned, and went to sleep again.

At last one morning the boat came to a stop. The excitement of change was in the air. François leashed the dogs and brought them on deck. At the first step upon the cold deck, Buck's feet sank into a white mushy something very like mud. He sprang back with a snort. More of this white stuff was falling through the air. He shook himself, but more of it fell upon him. He sniffed it curiously, then licked some up on his tongue. It bit like fire, and the next instant was gone. This puzzled him. He tried it again, with the same results. The men laughed, and he felt ashamed. This was the first time he had ever seen snow.

Buck's first day on the shore was like a nightmare. Every hour was filled with shock and surprise. No lazy, sunny life was this. Here there was no peace, nor rest, nor a moment's safety—only confusion and danger. Buck knew he must stay alert. These dogs and men were not town dogs and men. They were savages, all of them. They knew no law but the law of club and fang.

He had never seen dogs fight as these wolfish dogs fought. Buck soon learned an awful lesson about life in these wild parts—and Curly, the Newfoundland, was the victim.

They were camped near the log store, where Curly, in her friendly way, walked up to a husky dog the size of a full-grown wolf. With no warning, the husky leaped in like a flash, sank his teeth into Curly, then leaped back—almost in one motion.

It was the wolf way of fighting. Strike and leap away. Yet there was more to the wolf way than this. Thirty or forty huskies ran to the spot and surrounded the two dogs in a silent circle. Buck did not understand this silent circle, nor why they were licking their chops. Curly rushed the husky, who struck again and leaped aside. He met her next rush with his chest and tumbled her off her feet. She never got back up. This was what the circle of huskies had waited for. They closed in upon her, snarling and yelping in a mass attack. Within seconds, Curly was dead.

Buck was shocked by this sudden, brutal act. He saw Spitz stick out his red tongue in a way he had of laughing. Then he saw François, swinging an axe, spring into the mess of dogs. Three men with clubs were helping him to scatter them. It did not take long. The wild huskies were driven off and there lay Curly, limp and lifeless in the snow.

This memory often came back to Buck to trouble him in his sleep. So that was the way. No fair play. Once down, that was the end of you. Well, he would see to it that he never went down. Spitz stuck out his tongue and laughed again. From that moment Buck hated him with a bitter and deep hatred.

# CHAPTER FOUR

# The Team

Before long, Buck received another shock. François walked over to him with something made of leather straps. He then buckled and fastened this upon Buck. It was a harness.

Buck had often seen such harnesses put on horses back home on Judge Miller's estate. These horses were then put to work—something Buck had never been made to do. Yet now he was set to work pulling François on a sled to the forest for a load of firewood.

Buck had become a work animal. His pride suffered a blow. And though this was new and strange, he was determined to do his best.

Buck became the middle member of the three-dog sled team. He soon learned that order and teamwork were necessary. François was stern and taught the dogs to obey with his whip. Dave had worked on a team before and was an experienced "wheeler," holding the position closest to the sled. He nipped at Buck's hind legs whenever he was in error. Spitz was the lead dog. He growled sharply now and again and threw his weight into the two straps—the "traces"—that linked all the dogs.

Buck learned easily, and made good progress. Before they returned to camp, he knew enough to stop at "Ho," to go ahead at "Mush," to swing wide on the bends, and to keep clear of the wheeler when the loaded sled shot downhill at their heels.

"Three very good dogs," François told Perrault. "Dat Buck, him can pull! I teach him quick as anything."

By afternoon, Perrault returned with two more dogs. "Billee" and "Joe" he called them. They were brothers, and true huskies both, yet different as day and night. Billee was very friendly while Joe was sour and silent with an evil eye. Buck was friendly to both dogs and Dave ignored them. Spitz wanted to prove who was leader from the start. When Billee wagged his tail at Spitz, the white dog attacked him, sinking sharp teeth into the husky's flank. Then Spitz circled Joe. Billee had fled, but Joe whirled around on his heels to face Spitz—ears laid back, lips snarling, jaws clipping together, and eyes gleaming with stubborn fear.

By evening Perrault brought another dog, an old thin husky with only one good eye. He was called Sol-leks, which means "Angry One." Like Dave, he asked nothing, gave nothing, and commanded respect. Even Spitz left him alone. Sol-leks did not like to be approached on his blind side. Buck was unlucky enough to discover this. Sol-leks whirled upon Buck and slashed his shoulder to the bone when Buck walked up to the side with the bad eye. After this, Buck avoided his blind side, and had no more trouble.

That night Buck faced the great problem of sleeping out in the freezing cold. The tent was lit by a candle and it glowed warmly. Buck walked into the warm tent, but both Perrault and François yelled and threw plates and cups at him till he fled into the outer cold. He lay down on the snow and attempted to sleep, but he was shivering. Sadly he wandered about among the many tents. Each place was as cold as another.

Finally an idea came to him. He would return and see how his own teammates were making out. To his surprise, they had disappeared. Again he wandered about through the great camp, looking for them, and again he returned. Were they in the tent? No, that could not be, else he would not have been driven out. Then where could they possibly be? With drooping tail and shivering body he circled the tent. Suddenly the snow gave way beneath his forelegs and he sank down. Something wriggled under his feet. He sprang back, bristling and snarling. But a friendly little yelp calmed him and brought him back. There, curled up under the snow in a snug ball, lay Billee. He whined, squirmed, and wriggled to show his good will, and even licked Buck's face with his warm, wet tongue.

Another lesson. So that was the way they did it, eh? Buck selected a spot and, after a few tries, finally dug a hole for himself. The day had been long and hard. He slept soundly and comfortably, though he growled and barked and wrestled with bad dreams.

Buck did not open his eyes until he heard the sounds of the waking camp. At first he did not know where he was. It had snowed during the night and he was completely buried. The muscles of his whole body ached. The hair on his neck and shoulders stood on end. With a ferocious snarl, he bounded straight up into the open air, sending the snow flying. He landed on his feet and saw the camp. Then he remembered everything that had happened to him—from the stroll with Manuel, to the boat ride, to the sled team, to the hole he had dug for himself the night before.

"What I say?" the dog-driver François cried to Perrault. "Dat Buck for sure learn quick as anything."

Perrault nodded. The Canadian Government needed the best dogs on this run. He was glad to have Buck.

Three more huskies were added to the team, making a total of nine. Before long they were in harness and swinging up the trail away from the camp. Buck was glad to be gone. The work was hard, but he did not hate it. He was surprised at how much the other dogs enjoyed the work. They were all eager to get down the trail.

Dave was wheeler, or sled dog. Pulling in front of him was Buck. Then came Sol-leks. The rest of the team was strung out ahead, single file, to the leader—Spitz. Buck had been placed between Dave and Sol-leks to be taught the way of the team. When he needed instruction, he received a sharp nip or a pull in the traces.

That day they made forty miles on the snow-packed trail. The next few days they had to blaze a new trail, which was harder work and took more time. Perrault traveled ahead of the team, packing the snow with webbed shoes to make it easier for them. François usually guided the sled with the gee-pole. Perrault was in a hurry, but he knew the danger in rushing onto the thin autumn ice.

Day after day, Buck toiled in the traces. Always they broke camp in the dark of the early hours. At the first gray of dawn they were hitting the trail.

After dark the men pitched camp. The dogs ate their bit of fish, and crawled to sleep into the snow. Buck was starving. His pound and a half of sun-dried salmon was not enough food for his aching belly. The other dogs weighed less and were born to this life. A pound only of the fish kept them in good condition.

Buck watched and learned. When he saw Pike, one of the new dogs, slyly steal a slice of bacon when Perrault's back was turned, he copied the trick the following day, getting away with the whole chunk. An uproar was raised, but Buck was not suspected. Dub, who was always getting caught, was blamed and punished for Buck's misdeed.

Buck quickly grew strong and wise. His muscles became as hard as iron and he grew used to pain. He could eat anything, no matter how disgusting. He learned to bite the ice out with his teeth when it collected between his toes. When he was thirsty and the ice was thick over a water hole, he would strike and break it with stiff forelegs. His sense of smell and sense of hearing became very keen. His instincts came alive within him—the instincts of the wild, the instincts of his nature.

On the quiet, cold nights, he pointed his nose at a star and howled long and wolf-like. The "old song" of his ancient ancestors ran through him and he began to discover the primitive beast within him—a Buck he never knew— a Buck that had come alive all because men had found gold in the North, and because Manuel was a greedy man.

# CHAPTER FIVE

# The Primitive Beast

The "primitive beast" was strong in Buck and his life on the trail made it more and more dominant. He became cunning, with great poise and intelligence. He did not pick fights and he avoided them whenever possible. Even though he hated Spitz, he remained in control of his actions.

On the other hand, Spitz was always showing his teeth. He bullied Buck, trying to start the fight that could end only in the death of one or the other.

At the end of one hard day, they set up a quick camp on the shore of Lake Le Barge.

The wind cut like a white-hot knife. Darkness and the driving snow forced them to search for a camping place.

Under a sheltering rock, Buck made his nest in the snow. It was so snug and warm that he hated to leave it when François brought out a dinner of thawed fish. But when Buck finished his meal and returned, he found his nest occupied. There came a snarl from the trespasser—it was Spitz! Till now Buck had avoided trouble with his enemy, but this was too much. The beast in him roared. He sprang upon Spitz with a fury that surprised them both.

François was surprised, too, when both men rushed out to see the cause of the trouble.

"A-a-ah!" he cried to cheer on Buck. "Gif it to him! Gif it to him, the dirty thief!"

Spitz and Buck were circling each other with rage and caution. Then—suddenly—something happened that stopped the fight.

Perrault cried out and Buck heard the sound of a club and a shrill yelp of pain. The camp was alive with strange furry forms—a pack of starving huskies! There were eighty to one hundred of them. They had smelled the camp from some Indian village and were crazed by the smell of food.

In an instant the skinny brutes scrambled for the bread and bacon in a grub box. The men used their clubs with no effect. The wild dogs yelped and howled under the blows, but struggled madly till the last crumb was devoured.

The sled dogs burst out of their nests, only to be attacked by the fierce wild huskies. Never had Buck seen such dogs. They were like skeletons, with blazing eyes and frothing fangs, leaping toward the sled dogs. Buck's head and shoulders were ripped and slashed. Billee was crying as usual. Dave and Sol-leks dripped with blood, fighting bravely side by side. Joe snapped fiercely upon an invader's leg. Pike finished the job. Buck flung himself upon one, then another, till he felt teeth sink into his own throat. It was Spitz, attacking him from the side.

Perrault and François hurried to save their sled dogs. The wild, starving beasts fled and Buck shook himself free of Spitz. But it was only for a moment. The men then ran back to save the rest of the grub, and the huskies returned to attack the team. Billee sprang through the savage circle and fled away over the ice. Pike and Dub followed on his heels, with the rest of the team behind.

As Buck drew himself together to spring after them, out of the corner of his eye he saw Spitz rush upon him. He took the brunt of Spitz's charge, then joined the flight out on the frozen lake.

Later, the nine team-dogs gathered together in the forest. There was not one who was not wounded in four or five places. Dub was badly injured in a hind leg. Dolly, the last husky added to the team, had a badly torn throat. Joe had lost an eye. The good-natured Billee, with a ripped ear, cried and whimpered throughout the night. At daybreak they limped back to camp. The wild huskies had fled and the two men were in bad moods. Half their grub supply was gone. The huskies had chewed through the sled lashings. They had eaten a pair of Perrault's moose-hide moccasins, chunks out of the leather traces, and even two feet of lash from the end of François's whip. He looked up from the mess to see to his wounded dogs—wounded with the bites of huskies gone mad.

"Ah, my friends," he said softly, "mebbe it make you mad dog, those many bites. Mebbe all mad dog! What you think, eh, Perrault?"

Perrault shook his head. With four hundred miles of trail still between him and Dawson, he could not afford to have madness break out among his dogs. Two hours and much hard work later, the harnesses were repaired and the wounded team was under way. The hardest part of the trail between them and Dawson lay before them.

# CHAPTER SIX

# The Fight

It took six days of toil to cover thirty terrible miles. A dozen times Perrault, nosing the way, broke through the ice, being saved by the long pole he carried. Each time he broke through, he had to quickly build a fire to dry his garments. Once, the sled broke through—pulling Dave and Buck with it. They were half-frozen and all but drowned by the time they were dragged out. At another time Spitz went through, dragging the whole team after him up to Buck, who strained backward with all his strength. Behind him was Dave, straining backward, and behind the sled was François, pulling till his tendons cracked.

The entire team became exhausted. Perrault, to make up lost time, still pushed the tired dogs late and early.

Buck's feet were not so compact and hard as the feet of the huskies. All day long he limped in pain. At camp he lay down like a dead dog. He could not even move to get his dinner. François had to bring it to him. Perrault rubbed Buck's feet for half an hour each night after supper. He cut off the tops of his own moccasins to make four moccasins for Buck. This was a great relief. One morning François forgot the moccasins and Buck lay on his back, his four feet waving in the air. Perrault grinned at the sight of a dog that refused to budge without his "shoes." Later Buck's feet grew hard to the trail, and the worn-out footgear was thrown away.

One morning as they were harnessing up, Dolly went suddenly mad. Her long, sad wolf howl sent every dog bristling with fear. She then sprang straight for Buck. He had never seen a dog go mad, and he fled in a panic. Dolly, foaming at the mouth, ran wildly after Buck. At François's call, Buck circled back into camp. Here, the dog-driver waited with the axe which he brought down on the crazed, sick Dolly.

Buck staggered over to the sled, exhausted, sobbing for breath. This was Spitz's opportunity. He sprang upon Buck, and twice his teeth sank in and ripped the flesh to the bone. Then François's lash cracked, and Buck watched Spitz receive the worst whipping as yet given to any of the team.

"One devil, dat Spitz," remarked Perrault. "Some day him kill dat Buck."

"Dat Buck is two devils," was François's reply. "All de time I watch dat Buck, I know for sure. Listen… some fine day him get angry and den him chew dat Spitz all up. Sure, I know."

From then on it was war between Buck and Spitz. Spitz, as lead dog, had battled many dogs before. But Buck was different—he was smarter and more patient. Buck wanted the leadership position. He wanted it because it was his nature. He wanted it because he was gripped with a pride that matched the pride of Spitz.

One morning after a heavy snowfall, Pike did not appear. He was hidden in his nest under a foot of snow. François called for him but he still did not come. Spitz was wild with anger that a dog would disobey. He raged through the camp, smelling and digging until he found Pike in his hiding place.

Spitz flew at Pike to punish him. Just then, Buck flew with equal rage in between. Surprised, Spitz was hurled backward and off his feet. Pike joined the fight and Buck also sprang upon Spitz. But François, chuckling at the fight, brought his lash down upon Buck with all his might. Half-stunned, Buck was knocked backward and the lash fell upon him again and again, while Spitz soundly punished Pike.

In the days that followed, as Dawson grew closer and closer, Buck continued to interfere between Spitz and the other dogs. But he was crafty, waiting until François was not around. The team went from bad to worse. Things no longer went right. There was constant nipping and yelping—and at the bottom of it all was Buck. He kept François busy, watching out for the life-and-death struggle between Spitz and Buck that he knew would take place sooner or later.

They pulled into Dawson one dreary afternoon with the great fight still to come. Here were many men and countless dogs, all at work. All day they swung up and down the main street in long teams, and in the night their jingling bells still went by.

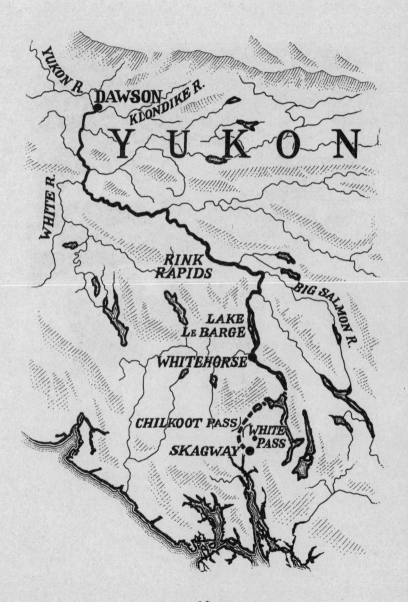

Here and there Buck met Southland dogs, like himself, but most were the wild wolf-husky breed. Every night, regularly at nine, at twelve, and three, they howled the eerie "old song." Buck joined them—the new Buck—the primordial beast.

The team rested for a day, then got back on the trail. They made splendid progress, but Buck kept stirring up trouble along the way. They no longer worked as "one dog" in the traces. Spitz was no longer a leader who was feared or respected. Pike robbed him of half a fish one night, and gulped it down under the protection of Buck. Another night Dub and Joe fought Spitz and watched him take the punishment that *they* deserved. And even Billee, the good-natured, grew more brave. Buck never came near Spitz without snarling and bristling.

François became furious with the team. His lash was always singing among the dogs, but it did little good. When his back was turned the dogs were at it again. François knew Buck was behind all of the trouble, and Buck knew François knew. Buck was too clever to ever again be caught red-handed.

One night after supper, Dub turned up a snowshoe rabbit and in a second the whole team was in full cry. A hundred yards away was a camp of the Northwest Police, with fifty huskies who joined the rabbit-chase. The rabbit sped down the river and turned off into a small creek, up the frozen bed. Buck led the pack, sixty strong, around bend after bend, but he could not gain. His splendid body flashed forward, leap by leap, in the pale white moonlight. And leap by leap the snowshoe rabbit flashed on ahead. Buck still led the pack, running the wild thing down.

But Spitz, cold and crafty, left the pack and cut across a piece of land along the creek. Buck did not know of this. As Buck rounded the bend, he saw a large, frosty shadow leap into the path of the rabbit. It was Spitz! The rabbit could not turn, and Spitz's white teeth seized it.

Buck made no sound, but drove in upon Spitz, shoulder to shoulder, so hard that he missed the throat. They rolled over and over in the powdery snow. Spitz gained his feet almost as though he had not been overthrown, slashing Buck's shoulder and leaping clear.

In a flash Buck knew it. The time had come. It was to the death. As they circled about, snarling, ears laid back, Buck's instincts took over. He seemed to remember it all—the white woods, and earth, and moonlight, and the thrill of battle. The air was silent and the wolf-huskies circled, their eyes gleaming.

Spitz knew how to fight, and whenever Buck lunged he was met with quicker fangs. Time and time again he leaped at Spitz, and each time Spitz slashed him and got away. Spitz was untouched, while Buck was streaming with blood and panting hard. The fight was growing desperate. Once Buck flipped over, and the whole circle of sixty dogs started up. But he recovered himself, almost in midair, and the circle sank down again... and waited.

Buck was smart—smarter than any dog Spitz had known. He rushed, pretending to go for the shoulder, but at the last instant he swept in low and closed on Spitz's left foreleg. The bone broke—and the white dog faced him on three legs. Buck tried again to knock him over, and then swept in to break the right foreleg. Despite the pain and helplessness, Spitz struggled to keep up.

But there was no hope for Spitz, and no mercy.

Buck readied for the final rush. A pause seemed to fall. Every animal stood still as though turned to stone. Then Buck sprang in—delivered the final bite—and sprang out. No more would Spitz stand in his way. Buck was again a king.

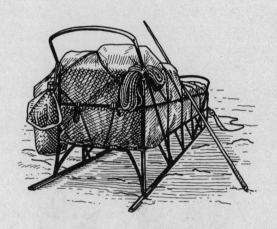

# CHAPTER SEVEN

# Who Will Lead?

"Eh? What I say? I speak true when I say dat Buck two devils," said François the next morning.

"Dat Spitz fight like the devil," said Perrault, as he looked over the rips and cuts.

"An' dat Buck fight like *two* devils," was François's answer. "And now we make good time. No more Spitz, no more trouble, sure."

Perrault packed up and loaded the sled while François started to harness the dogs. Buck trotted up to the place Spitz used to hold as leader. François, not noticing him, brought Sol-leks to the lead. Buck sprang upon Sol-leks in a fury, driving him back and standing in his place.

"Eh? Eh?" François cried, slapping his thighs gleefully. "Look at dat Buck. Him kill dat Spitz, him think to take de job. Go 'way, now, Buck!"

Buck refused to budge.

He took Buck by the scruff of the neck, dragged him to one side, and put Sol-leks back in the lead. The old dog did not like it—he was afraid of Buck. When François turned his back, Buck again made Sol-leks step aside.

François was angry. "Now, by darn, I fix you!" he cried, coming back with a heavy club in his hand.

Buck remembered the man in the red sweater, and backed away slowly. He did not charge in when Sol-leks was once more put in the lead. He circled, just beyond reach of the club, snarling with rage.

The driver went about his work. He called to Buck when he was ready to put him in his old place in front of Dave. Buck took two or three steps back. François followed him up. Buck retreated again. After some time of this, François threw down the club, thinking that Buck feared a thrashing. But Buck was in open revolt. He wanted to be the leader. It was his by right.

He had earned it, and he would not be content with less.

Perrault came to help, but for an hour the two men could not get Buck into position. They threw clubs at him. He dodged. They yelled at him, and he snarled and kept out of their reach. He did not try to run away, but retreated around and around the camp.

François sat down and scratched his head. Perrault angrily looked at his watch. Time was flying. They should have been on the trail an hour ago. François scratched his head again. He shook it and grinned at Perrault, who shrugged his shoulders. Then François went up to where Sol-leks stood and called to Buck. Buck laughed, as dogs laugh, yet kept his distance. François unfastened Sol-leks's traces and put him back in his old place. The team stood harnessed and ready for the trail, with only one open spot—the lead position.

François called and Buck trotted in, laughing in triumph. He swung around into position at the head of the team. His traces were fastened, the sled was broken out, and with both men running they dashed out onto the river trail.

Buck proved to be an excellent leader. He kept order among the dogs and kept the team moving at a fast pace. Dave and Sol-leks did not mind the change in leadership. They loved the work—the toil in the traces—and Buck worked them hard. The rest of the team had grown unruly during Spitz's last days, and they were surprised at how Buck got them all into shape.

Pike, who pulled at Buck's heels, was used to being lazy. Buck swiftly punished him, and, before the first day was done, Pike was pulling more than ever before in his life. The first night in camp, Joe, the sour one, was disciplined with bites and snarls. Buck let the team know who was boss—and the team improved greatly. Once more the dogs leaped as "one dog" in the traces.

At the Rink Rapids, two native huskies— Teek and Koona—were added. Buck broke them so quickly it took away François's breath.

"Never such a dog as dat Buck!" he cried. "No, never! Him worth one thousand dollars, for sure! Eh? What you say, Perrault?"

And Perrault nodded. He was ahead of the record then, and gaining day by day. The trail was in excellent condition, well packed and hard.

There was no new soft snow, and it was not too cold. The men rode and ran by turn, and the dogs were kept on the jump. On the last night of the second week, they topped White Pass and dropped down the sea slope toward Skagway.

It was a record run. Each day for fourteen days they had averaged forty miles. When they reached Skagway, the team became the center of attention by a crowd of dogbusters and mushers.

The mission was now complete. The two Canadians had new orders that required a fresh team of dogs. François called Buck to him, threw his arms around him, and wept good-bye. And that was the last of François and Perrault. Like other men, they passed out of Buck's life for good.

# CHAPTER EIGHT

# The Toil of the Trail

A mail carrier, a Scotch half-breed, took charge of Buck's team, along with a dozen other dog teams. The sleds were loaded up with sacks of mail, and the dogs started back over the weary trail to Dawson. The running was hard now. The loads were heavy. There was toil each day. There were no record times.

Buck did not like it, but he pulled hard and took pride in his work—just like Dave and Solleks did. As leader, he made sure that every dog did his fair share of the work.

It was a boring life. One day was very much like another. At a certain time each morning,

the cooks turned out, fires were built, and breakfast was eaten. Then, while some broke camp, others harnessed the dogs, and they were under way an hour or so before dawn. At night, camp was made. Some pitched the tents, others cut firewood and collected pine branches for the beds. Still others carried water or ice for the cooks. Then the dogs were fed their meal of fish. This was the one time of day when the team could relax for an hour or so with the other dogs.

Best of all, Buck loved to lie near the fire with his eyes blinking dreamily at the flames. Sometimes he thought of Judge Miller's big house in the sunny Santa Clara Valley, and of the swimming tank. But more often he remembered the man in the red sweater, the death of Curly, the great fight with Spitz, and the good things he had eaten or would like to eat. He was not homesick. His old home was a very dim and distant memory. Far more powerful were his instincts. These new instincts seemed to come from ancestors long ago—from a time when the dog was a wild breed running with a wilder sort of man.

Sometimes as he crouched there, blinking at the flames, it seemed that the flames were of another fire. As if in a dream, he saw a different man from the Canadian cook in front of him. This other man had short, muscular legs and long arms. The hair was long and matted. He uttered strange sounds, and seemed very much afraid of the darkness as he peered into it. He clutched a stick with a heavy stone at one end. He was a hairy, primitive man—a primordial man. He did not stand up straight, but leaned forward from the hips on legs that bent at the knees—as if ready to pounce out of fear.

At other times this hairy man squatted by the fire with his head between his legs and slept. And beyond that fire, in the darkness, Buck could see many gleaming eyes, always two by two, which he knew to be the eyes of great beasts of prey. And he could hear the crashing of their bodies through the undergrowth, and the noises they made in the night.

These sounds and sights of this dream-like world would make the hair rise along his back. He would whimper low or growl softly, and the cook would shout at him, "Hey, you Buck, wake up!"

Then the other world would vanish and the real world would come into his eyes. He would get up and yawn and stretch as though he had been asleep.

The loads of mail were heavy and this was a hard trip. The work wore the dogs down. They were in poor condition when they finally pulled into Dawson, and should have had a week-long rest. But within two days' time they were loaded up again to take more mail loads. The dogs were tired, the drivers grumbled, and, to make matters worse, it snowed every day. This meant a soft trail and heavier pulling for the dogs. The drivers were fair through it all, and did their best for the dogs.

Each night the dogs were attended to first. They ate before the drivers ate, and no man went to sleep without first checking on the feet of the dogs he drove. Still, their strength went down. Since the beginning of the winter, they had traveled nearly 2000 miles, dragging sleds the whole weary distance. Buck stood it, leading his team well, though he too was very tired. Billee cried and whimpered in his sleep each night. Joe was more sour than ever, and Sol-leks only wanted to be left alone.

But it was Dave who suffered most of all. He became more sad and irritable. When camp was pitched, he made his nest at once, where his driver fed him. He did not get on his feet again till harness-up time in the morning. He often cried out in pain in the traces. The driver examined him, but could find nothing. All the drivers became interested in his case. They talked it over at meal time. He was brought from his nest to the fire and was pressed and prodded till he cried out many times. Something was wrong inside him, but they could find no broken bones.

By the time they reached Cassiar Bar, he was so weak that again and again he fell in the traces. The Scotch mail carrier called a halt and took him out of the team, making the next dog, Sol-leks, the new wheeler next to the sled. He wanted to give Dave a rest and let him run free behind the sled. Sick as he was, Dave would have no part of this. He growled while his traces were removed. He whimpered broken-heartedly when he saw Sol-leks in the position he had held and served so long. His pride was hurt—and this was more painful than his illness. He could not bear that another dog should do his work.

When the sled started, Dave ran alongside the team, trying to get back into his place, crying with grief and pain. The driver whipped him, but he paid no attention to the stings. The man didn't have the heart to strike harder. Dave struggled to run behind the sled. Then he fell howling as the long train of sleds went by. With the last bit of his strength he managed to stagger along behind until the train made another stop. He somehow reached his own sled and stood alongside Sol-leks.

His driver stopped a moment to get a light for his pipe. Then he returned and started his dogs. They swung out on the trail with no effort at all—but then stopped in surprise. The driver was surprised, too. The sled had not moved! He called the other men over to see the strange sight. *Dave had bitten through both of Sol-leks' traces*, and was standing directly in front of the sled in his proper place.

The dog pleaded with his eyes to remain there. Since Dave was dying, the men agreed that he should die in the traces where he wanted to be. So he was harnessed in, and he proudly pulled again, though more than once he cried out from a pain within him.

He held out till camp was reached and his driver made a place for him by the fire. In the morning he was too weak to travel. His strength had left him and he was dying. He could not be harnessed, and the team went on without him. The whips snapped, the bells jingled merrily, the sleds churned along the trail.

Buck knew, and every dog knew, they would never see Dave again.

# CHAPTER NINE

# The Tenderfeet

Thirty days from the time they left Dawson, Buck and his team arrived at Skagway. They were worn out and worn down. Buck's one hundred and forty pounds had gone down to one hundred and fifteen. The rest of his mates had lost weight, too. Pike limped with a hurt leg. Sol-leks was also limping, and Dub was suffering from a hurt shoulder blade. The dogs were all very footsore. Their feet plodded along with no joy for the work. The months of constant toil left them with no strength. It had all been used. Every muscle, every fiber, every cell was tired—dead tired. And there was reason for it.

In less than five months they had traveled 2500 miles with little or no rest. When they arrived at Skagway, they were on their last legs.

"Mush on, poor sore feets," the driver said as they slowly staggered down the main street of Skagway. "This is de last. Then we get one long rest, eh? For sure. One long rest."

The drivers expected a long stopover. They deserved a rest and a chance to relax. But there were so many men who had rushed to the Klondike in search of gold that the mail loads had increased. Fresh teams of dogs were brought in to take the places of the worn-out teams. These worthless dog teams were no longer useful on the mail runs—and so these teams were sold.

After only three days of rest, Buck's team— harness and all—was bought by two men from the United States. The men called each other "Hal" and "Charles." Charles was a man about age forty, with watery eyes and a mustache that twisted up. Hal was a young man of nineteen or twenty, with a big revolver and a hunting knife strapped to his belt. Both men were out of place. They were "tenderfeet"—newcomers who did not know the ways of the wild North.

The new owners' camp was a mess. The tent was put up poorly and the dishes were not washed. There was also a woman with them called "Mercedes." She was Charles's wife and Hal's sister. Three tenderfeet in one family.

Buck watched the two men take the camp apart and load the sled. They did not know how to roll the tent. The tin dishes were packed away unwashed. Mercedes kept complaining and giving advice to Hal and Charles. They packed and unpacked several times, never getting things "just right" for Mercedes.

Three men from a neighboring tent came out and looked on, grinning and winking at one another.

"You've got a right big load as it is," said one of them. "It's not for me to say, but I wouldn't tote that tent along if I was you."

"Nonsense!" cried Mercedes. "However in the world could I manage without a tent?"

"It's springtime, ma'am, and you won't get any more cold weather," the man replied.

She shook her head at the men.

"Ya think that sled will ride?" one of the men asked.

"Why shouldn't it?" Charles demanded.

"I was just a-wondering, that is all. It seemed a mite top-heavy," said the man.

Charles turned his back and tied the bundles down as best he could—which was rather sloppily.

"And of course the dogs can hike all day with that top-heavy load, eh?" came another comment.

"Certainly," said Hal. He took hold of the gee-pole with one hand and the whip with the other. "Mush!" he shouted. "Mush on there!"

The dogs sprang forward, strained hard for a few moments, then relaxed. They were unable to move the sled.

"The lazy brutes! I'll show them," Hal cried, raising his whip.

But Mercedes cried, "Oh, Hal, you mustn't!" She caught hold of the whip and pulled it from him. "The poor dears! Now, you must promise you won't be harsh with them for the rest of the trip, or I won't go a step."

"You know nothing about dogs," her brother sneered, "and I wish you'd leave me alone. They're lazy, I tell you, and you've got to whip them to get anything out of them. That's their way. You ask anyone. Ask one of those men."

Mercedes looked at the men.

"They're much too weak, if you want to know," replied one. "Plumb tuckered out, that's what's the matter. They need a rest."

"Rest indeed," snarled Hal.

"Never mind that man," Mercedes said. "You're driving our dogs and you do what you think best with them."

Again Hal's whip fell upon the dogs. They threw themselves forward, dug their feet into the packed snow, got down low to it, and put forth all their strength. The sled would not move. After two efforts, they stood still, panting. Hal's whip kept singing. Mercedes stopped the whipping, dropped on her knees before Buck, and with tears in her eyes, put her arms around his neck.

"You poor, poor dears," she cried, "why don't you pull hard? Then you wouldn't be whipped." Buck did not like her.

An onlooker spoke up. "I don't care a whoop what becomes of *you*, but for the dogs' sakes I just want to tell you this. You can help them a mighty lot by breaking out that sled. The runners are frozen in the icy snow. Throw your weight against the gee-pole, right and left, and *break* it out."

After a third try, Hal broke out the runners which had been frozen in the snow. The dogs managed to pull the overloaded sled down the path. But when the path turned onto the main street, the top-heavy sled went over, spilling half its load.

The dogs never stopped—the sled bounded on its side behind them. Buck was raging at the whippings they had received. He broke into a run and the team followed his lead.

"Whoa! Whoa!" Hal cried out. He tripped and was pulled off his feet.

The dogs dashed on up the street as they scattered the remainder of the gear along the main street of Skagway.

The dogs and the scattered gear and clothes were rounded up.

"You need just half the load and twice the dogs, if you ever expect to reach Dawson," the men told Charles, Hal, and Mercedes.

Mercedes cried while she went through clothes, deciding what to keep. Although they went through every article until the load was cut in half, it was still too bulky.

Charles and Hal went out that evening and bought six "Outsider" dogs. This brought their team up to fourteen. But the newcomer dogs did not amount to much. They did not seem to know anything. Buck speedily taught them their places and what *not* to do, but he could not teach them what *to* do. They did not take kindly to trace and trail.

The two men were quite proud and cheerful as they set off down the trail with fourteen dogs—fourteen dogs not ready for the hard work ahead. Eight dogs were dead-tired and six dogs had never pulled a sled. But fourteen dogs they had! They had never seen a sled with so many as *fourteen dogs*!

In the Arctic, there was a reason why fourteen dogs should not drag one sled. This was that *one sled* could not carry the food needed for *fourteen dogs*. But Charles and Hal did not know this. They had worked the trip out with a pencil—so much to a dog, so many dogs, and so many days. It was all so *very* simple.

Buck felt that he could not depend upon these two men and the woman. They did not know how to do anything and did not want to learn.

They were lazy. It took them half the night to pitch camp, and half the morning to break that camp and get the sled loaded. Yet the work was so sloppy that for the rest of the day they had to stop to rearrange the load. Some days they did not make ten miles. On other days they were unable to get started at all. And all the while, the food supply was going down.

# CHAPTER TEN

## Hitting the Bottom

Of course they ran short on dog food.

Charles and Hal overfed the dogs at first. The six Outsider dogs had big appetites. Mercedes, with tears in her pretty eyes, could not get Charles to give the dogs more, so she stole from the fish sacks and fed them secretly. But it was not food that Buck and the huskies needed most—it was rest. And though they were making poor time, the heavy load they dragged took all their strength away.

Then the underfeeding began.

Hal realized one day that his dog food was half gone and they had covered very little distance.

They could not get more dog food, so he cut down on even the usual amount and tried to increase the day's travel. It was easy to give the dogs less food, but it was impossible to make the dogs travel faster. The men didn't know how to work dogs—they didn't even know how to work themselves.

The first to go was Dub. Poor thief that he was, always getting caught and punished, he had still been a faithful worker. The Outsider dogs did not last long. One by one they died.

By this time there was no joy in this Arctic adventure for any of the three people. Mercedes no longer wept over the dogs. She only wept over herself—except when she was quarreling with her husband and brother. And the three did quarrel. They were stiff and in pain. Their muscles ached, their bones ached, their very hearts ached. They had only hard words for each other. In the meantime, the fire remained unbuilt, the camp half-pitched, and the dogs unfed.

They thought only of their own misery and gave no thought to the animals. Through it all, Buck staggered along at the head of the starved team as if in a nightmare. He pulled when he could. When he could no longer pull, he fell down

and remained down till blows from whip or club drove him to his feet again. His once beautiful fur was dull and matted. He had become so thin that each rib and every bone in his body showed through his loose hide. It was heartbreaking—yet Buck's heart was unbreakable. The man in the red sweater had proved that many months before.

Buck's team of six dogs looked like skeletons. They no longer felt the pain of the whip, and their eyes looked lifeless. When the team stopped, they dropped down in the traces like dead dogs, with no spark left. When the club or whip fell upon them, the spark somehow fluttered, and they tottered to their feet and staggered on.

There came a day when Billee, the good-natured, fell and could not rise. Buck and the others knew their own time would be soon. On the next day, Koona went, and only five of them remained. Joe was too ill to be mean. Pike was crippled and limping. Sol-leks, the one-eyed, was still faithful to his work—even in his agony. Teek, who had not traveled so far that winter, had been beaten more than the others. And Buck was still at the head of the team, but he was too weak to lead the starved, weary dogs.

The dogs were falling. Mercedes was weeping and riding. Hal and Charles were arguing. This was what they were doing when they staggered into John Thornton's camp at the mouth of the White River. When they stopped, the dogs dropped down as though they had all been struck dead. Mercedes dried her eyes and looked at John Thornton. Charles sat down on a log to rest. Hal did the talking. John Thornton was whittling an axe-handle. He whittled and listened, gave short replies and very little advice. He knew this type of traveler, and he knew they would not listen to advice.

John Thornton *did* tell them *not* to take chances on the ice. Hal waved his hand toward the frozen White River.

"They told us up in Skagway that we couldn't make White River, and here we are," said Hal with a jeer. "They said we should stay away from travel over ice, but we made it."

"And they told you true," John Thornton answered. "The ice is likely to bottom out at any moment. Only lucky fools could have made it. I tell you straight, I wouldn't risk my life on that ice for all the gold in Alaska."

"That's because you're not a fool, I suppose," said Hal. "All the same, we'll go on to Dawson." He took out his whip. "Get up there, Buck! Hi! Get up there! Mush on!"

Thornton went on whittling. He knew these fools would not listen.

But the team did not get up at the command and so the whip flashed out. John Thornton watched in silence. Sol-leks was the first to crawl to his feet. Teek followed. Joe came next, yelping with pain. Pike made painful efforts. Twice he fell over, when half-up, and on the third attempt managed to rise.

Buck made no effort. He lay quietly where he had fallen. The lash bit into him again and again. He did not whine or struggle. Several times Thornton started to speak, but changed his mind. Tears came to his eyes as the whipping went on.

This was the first time Buck had failed, and this angered Hal. No matter how he beat Buck, the poor dog would not budge. All day Buck had felt the thin, rotten ice under his feet. He sensed that danger lay ahead. He refused to stir. He felt numb. He no longer felt pain. He was slipping away.

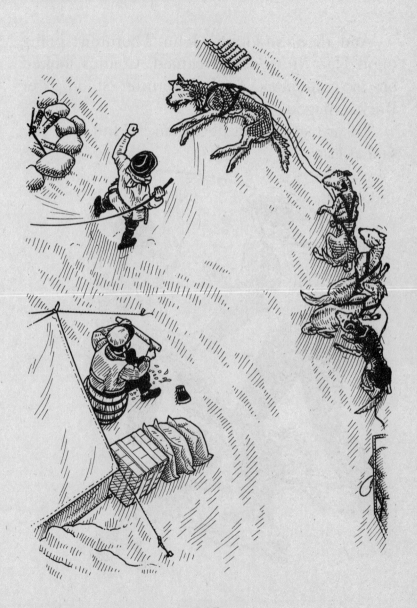

And then, suddenly, John Thornton sprang upon Hal. Mercedes screamed. Charles looked on in confusion. John Thornton stood over Buck, enraged.

"If you strike that dog again, I'll kill you," he said at last.

"It's my dog," Hal replied. "Get out of my way, or I'll fix you. I'm going to Dawson."

Thornton stood between him and Buck, and would not get out of the way. Hal drew his long hunting knife, but Thornton rapped Hal's knuckles with his axe handle, knocking the knife to the ground. Then he picked up the knife himself, and with two strokes cut Buck's traces.

Hal gave up on Buck—what use was he anymore, anyway? A few minutes later the tenderfeet pulled out from the bank and out onto the frozen river. Buck heard them go and raised his head to see. Pike was leading, Sol-leks was at the wheel, and between were Joe and Teek. They were limping and staggering. Mercedes was riding the loaded sled. Hal guided at the gee-pole, and Charles stumbled along at the back.

As Buck watched them, Thornton knelt beside him and petted him with rough but kind hands. Dog and man both watched the sled crawling along over the ice. Suddenly, they saw its back end drop down and the gee-pole jerk into the air. Mercedes screamed. They saw Charles turn one step to run back. Then a whole section of ice gave way and dogs and humans disappeared.

A white hole in the ice was all that was to be seen. The bottom had dropped out of the trail.

John Thornton and Buck looked at each other.

"You poor devil," said John Thornton, and Buck licked his hand.

# CHAPTER ELEVEN

# For the Love of a Man

When John Thornton's feet froze last December, his partners made sure he was comfortable before they left to get a raft in Dawson. He was still limping slightly at the time he rescued Buck. Together man and dog lay by the riverbank through the long spring days, watching the running water, listening to the songs of birds and the hum of nature. John Thornton improved and Buck slowly won back his strength.

Buck could now be lazy as his wounds healed and his muscles came back to cover his bones. John Thornton's two dogs, Skeet and Night,

befriended Buck. Skeet was a little Irish setter who washed and cleansed Buck's wounds. Each morning after he had finished his breakfast, she attended to him. Night was a huge black dog, half-bloodhound and half-deerhound, with eyes that laughed with a good nature.

To Buck's surprise, these dogs showed no jealousy toward him. They seemed to share the kind nature of John Thornton. As Buck grew stronger they coaxed him into all sorts of ridiculous games, with John Thornton joining in. Buck romped through his time of healing and discovered a new feeling. Love. Real love for the first time. He had never really felt this before—not even for Judge Miller. But now, Buck came to love and adore John Thornton.

This man had saved his life. More than this, he was the ideal master. Other men had fed him and taken care of his needs, but John Thornton took care of his dogs as if they were his own children—because he truly cared. He never forgot to give a kind greeting or a cheering word. To sit down for a long talk with them was as much his delight as theirs.

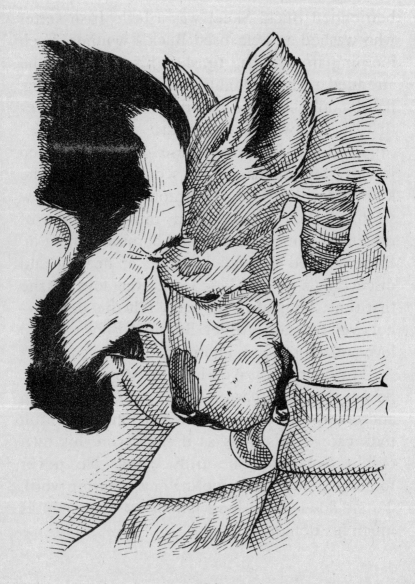

He had a way of taking Buck's head roughly between his hands and, resting his own head upon Buck's, playfully shaking him back and forth. He growled names at him and cursed him lovingly. "You mean old rascal," Thornton would say. Buck found joy in this playful embrace, and, when the man released him, Buck sprang to his feet with his mouth and eyes laughing. John Thornton would exclaim, "Buck, you can all but speak!"

Buck expressed his love to this man in his own way. He would often seize Thornton's hand in his mouth and hold tight—biting hard enough to leave marks. Yet the man understood, wrestling the dog with spirit and joy.

Most of the time, however, Buck was content to adore from a distance. He went wild with happiness when Thornton touched him or spoke to him, but he did not seek this attention. Skeet liked to shove her nose under Thornton's hand and nudge and nudge till she was petted. Night would often walk up and rest his great head on Thornton's knee. But Buck was happy just to lie at Thornton's feet for hours, looking up into his face.

He studied the man's expressions and move-
ments. And often, John Thornton would sense
Buck's gaze and would turn to gaze back at the
dog, without speech, his heart shining out of his
eyes as Buck's heart shone out, too.

For a long time after his rescue, Buck did not want Thornton to be out of his sight. From the moment he left the tent to when he entered it again, Buck would follow at his heels. He was afraid that Thornton would pass out of his life as Perrault and François and the mail carriers had passed out. Even in the night, in his dreams, he was haunted by this fear. At such times he would creep through the chilly air to the flap of the tent, where he would stand and listen to the sound of his master's breathing.

But in spite of this great love for John Thornton, Buck's primitive nature remained strong within him. He was faithful and devoted to this man who had saved his life, but he could never be tamed again. The cruelty of other men and months on the trail had changed him forever. Deep inside, he was a thing of the wild, come in from the wild to sit by John Thornton's fire. Because of his very great love, he could not steal from this man, but from any *other* man, in any *other* camp, he did not hesitate to steal. His keen intelligence and primitive instincts were strong.

His face and body were marked by the teeth of many dogs, and he still fought as fiercely as ever.

Skeet and Night were too good-natured for quarreling—besides, they belonged to John Thornton. But any strange dog, no matter what the breed, swiftly gave in to Buck. He had learned well the law of club and fang, and he never showed mercy to any other dog. He had learned well from Spitz—show no weakness, fight to the end. The strongest dog who showed no fear would rule. Buck knew this all too well.

Deep in the forest, and deep within him, a call was sounding. Even as he lay by John Thornton's warm safe fire, he heard this call. Then he would turn his back upon the fire and plunge into the forest. He would run—on and on—though he knew not where or why. He did not wonder where or why, so strong was the call. But each time, the love for John Thornton drew him back to the fire again.

Thornton was the only man Buck could love. Sometimes travelers praised or petted Buck, but he would often get up and walk away. When Thornton's partners, Hans and Pete, arrived on the raft, Buck refused to notice them till he learned they were close friends with Thornton. Even then, along the entire raft trip up to Dawson, he mostly ignored these other men.

For Thornton, however, his love seemed to grow and grow. He, alone among men, could put a pack upon Buck's back for the summer traveling. Nothing was too great for Buck to do when Thornton commanded.

"It's uncanny how Thornton and that dog seem to speak to each other," Pete noted one day.

"By Jingo, you are right," Hans answered. "Dat dog—him do anyt'ing for dat man. I hope no man ever get in the way between dem."

# CHAPTER TWELVE

# The Sled Pull

In Dawson that winter, Buck showed this uncanny loyalty and love for John Thornton.

The three partners had stopped off at a saloon one evening. "Black" Burton was there—an evil-tempered bully—and he was picking a fight with a young tenderfoot. Trying to hold tempers down, Thornton stepped in between. Buck, as was his custom, was lying in a corner of the room, head on paws, watching his master's every action. Black Burton struck out, without warning, and hit Thornton. He was sent spinning, and he saved himself from falling only by clutching the rail of the bar.

Those who were looking on heard something—not a bark nor a yelp—but something like a roar. They saw Buck's body rise up in the air as he left the floor for Burton's throat. The man saved his life by blocking with his arm, but was hurled backward with Buck on top of him. Then the crowd was upon Buck, and he was driven off.

While a doctor attended to Burton, Buck prowled up and down, growling, trying to rush in. Only heavy clubs could drive him back. A meeting was called on the spot, and all agreed that the dog had a just cause for attacking Burton. He was allowed to leave with Thornton, but his reputation was made. From that day, his name spread through every camp in Alaska.

Buck, because of his fame, was often compared to other dogs, and Thornton was driven to defend him. When the subject of dogs came up at the Eldorado Saloon one night, several men boasted of their favorites. At the end of half an hour, one man stated that *his* dog could start a sled with five hundred pounds and walk off with it. A second man bragged six hundred for *his* dog. A third, a man named Matthewson, boasted that *his* dog could start seven hundred.

"Hah!" said John Thornton. "Buck can start a thousand pounds."

"And break it out of the snow, and walk off with it for a hundred yards?" demanded Matthewson.

"And break it out, and walk off with it for a hundred yards," replied John Thornton.

"Well," Matthewson said slowly, so that all could hear, "I've got a thousand dollars that says he can't. And there it is." He slammed a sack of gold dust down upon the bar.

Nobody spoke. Thornton could feel a flush of warm blood creeping up his face. He did not know whether Buck could start a thousand pounds. Half a ton! He had great faith in Buck's strength, but how could he put Buck up to such a task? Plus, he didn't have a thousand dollars, and nor did Hans or Pete. The eyes of a dozen men fixed upon him, silent and waiting.

"I've got a sled standing outside right now with twenty fifty-pound sacks of flour on it," Matthewson went on. "We can put your dog to the test any time."

Thornton did not reply. He did not know what to say. He glanced from face to face, trying to gather his thoughts.

The face of Jim O'Brien, an old friend, caught Thornton's eyes. "Can you lend me a thousand?" he asked Jim, almost in a whisper.

"Sure," answered O'Brien, thumping down a sack next to Matthewson's. "Though I don't think, John, that the dog can do the trick."

The saloon emptied into the street. Several hundred men gathered to watch and bet on the outcome. Matthewson's sled, loaded with a thousand pounds of flour, had been standing for a couple of hours and the sled-runners had frozen fast to the hard-packed snow. Not a man believed the dog could even budge the sled, and they all bet against Buck.

Thornton looked at the sled itself, with the regular team of ten dogs still in harness. He had hurried into this foolishly and the task looked impossible. Matthewson, on the other hand, was quite pleased. "Three to one odds!" he proclaimed. "I'll bet you another thousand dollars, Thornton, what do you say?"

Thornton's doubt was strong, but so were his pride and his fighting spirit—the fighting spirit that does not care about the odds, that does not believe something is impossible.

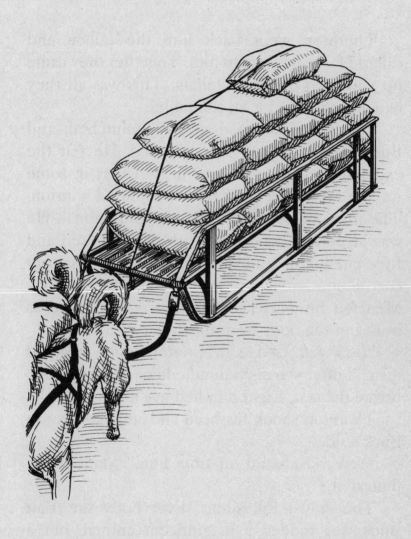

Thornton went back into the saloon and called Hans and Pete to him. Together they came up with two hundred dollars. This was all they had, yet they laid it on the table.

The team of ten dogs was unhitched, and Buck was harnessed into the sled. He felt the excitement in the air, and he felt that in some way he must do a great thing for John Thornton. The men took note of this splendid animal. He was in perfect condition, with one hundred and fifty pounds of pure muscle and grit. His furry coat shone and every hair seemed to be alive. Men felt his muscles, proclaimed them hard as iron, and the odds went down to two to one.

"Gad, sir! Gad, sir!" stuttered one bearded man. "I offer you eight hundred dollars for him, sir, before the test. Eight hundred just as he stands."

Thornton shook his head and stepped over to Buck's side.

"You must stand off from him," Matthewson protested.

The crowd fell silent. Everybody saw that Buck was indeed a magnificent animal, but a thousand pounds—how could he break out and pull such a load?

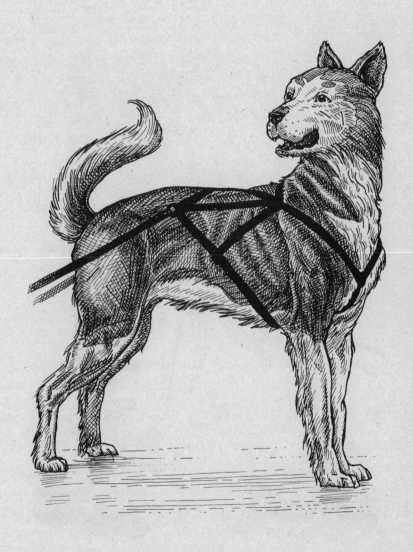

Thornton knelt down by Buck's side. He took his head in his hands and rested cheek on cheek. He did not playfully shake him, as he usually did, or tease him with words. Instead he just whispered in his ear, "As you love me, Buck. As you love me." Buck whined with an eagerness to please.

The crowd was watching curiously. This was odd—a man whispering to a dog. As Thornton got to his feet, Buck seized his mittened hand between his jaws, pressing in with his teeth and then letting go. It was the answer—not of speech, but of love. Thornton stepped well back.

"Now, Buck," he said.

Buck tightened the traces, then let them loosen a bit. It was the way he had learned.

"*Gee!*" Thornton's voice rang out sharply.

Buck swung to the right with all his might. The load quivered, and from under the runners arose a crisp crackling.

"*Haw!*" Thornton commanded.

Buck pulled this time to the left. The crackling turned into a snapping. The runners slipped several inches to the side. The sled was broken out! Every man was holding his breath.

"Now, *MUSH!*"

Thornton's command cracked out like a pistol shot. Buck threw himself forward. His whole body—and every muscle—went into the effort. His great chest was low to the ground, his head forward and down, while his feet were flying like mad, the claws digging into the hard-packed snow. The sled swayed slightly. One of Buck's feet slipped, and one man groaned aloud. The sled jerked ahead... half an inch... an inch... two inches... The jerks became fewer until the sled was moving ahead slowly, slowly, steadily...

Men gasped and began to breathe again. Thornton was running behind, encouraging Buck with short, cheery words. As he neared the pile of firewood that marked the end of the hundred yards, a cheer began to grow and grow, which burst into a roar as he passed the firewood and halted at command. Every man began to jump with joy and wonder—even Matthewson. Hats and mittens were flying in the air. Men were shaking hands and bubbling over in a general excitement.

But Thornton fell on his knees beside Buck. Head was against head, and he was shaking him back and forth. Those close by heard him

roughing it up and growling words at Buck, softly and lovingly. "You old rascal. You darned old rascal!"

"I'll give you a thousand dollars for him, sir, a thousand, sir!" exclaimed the bearded man.

Thornton rose to his feet. His eyes were wet. The tears were streaming down his cheeks. "Sir," he said, "no, sir. You can forget it, sir."

Buck seized Thornton's hand in his teeth. Thornton shook him back and forth. Man and dog romped, alone within their special love for each other, while all the men looked on in wonder.

# CHAPTER THIRTEEN

# The Sounding of the Call

Sixteen hundred dollars! Buck earned John Thornton enough money to travel with his partners into the East in search of a "lost" gold mine. Many men had looked for it. Few had found it. And many had never returned from their search. Yet there were stories that told of this lost mine near an old cabin—a mine with the most fantastic gold nuggets.

John Thornton, Pete, and Hans, with Buck and six other dogs, went in search of this old cabin and this treasure. John Thornton was not afraid of the wild. He was at home on any trail. He hunted for food and traveled light.

To Buck it was a great life, this hunting, fishing, and wandering through strange places. The months came and went. They faced blizzards and bitter cold in the winter months and gnats and flies in the warm months. They rafted across blue mountain lakes, and drifted down rivers in slender boats carved from tree trunks. Sometimes they went hungry, sometimes they feasted. This was adventure!

And through another winter they wandered. Then spring came on once more, and at the end of all their wandering they found not the "lost mine and old cabin," but a shallow placer—a deposit of gravel where gold is often found. Here the gold showed like yellow butter across the bottom of the washing pan!

Each day they worked they earned thousands of dollars in clean dust and nuggets, and they worked every day. The gold was sacked in moose-hide bags, fifty pounds to the bag. With no more thought of the "lost mine," they heaped their treasure up.

There was very little for the dogs to do, and Buck spent long hours by the fire. The vision of the short-legged hairy man came to him more often.

Buck gazed into the fire and could see the hairy man—as if in a dream—living with fear in that other world.

He watched the hairy man sleeping by the fire, crouched with his hands over his head in fear. Sometimes Buck dreamed that they walked on a beach, gathering shellfish. Even then, the hairy man was alert to hidden danger, ready to run like the wind.

Buck felt the wild stirrings of his own soul. The visions of the hairy man told him of the days of his ancestors. But the sounds and calls from the forest told him of a new life waiting now. Sometimes he followed the call into the forest, looking for it, barking softly. He would thrust his nose into the earth and moss. He would crouch for hours, wide-eyed and wide-eared to all that moved and sounded about him.

When the call came to him, he listened. He would be dozing lazily in camp when suddenly his head would lift and his ears cock up, listening. He would spring to his feet and dash away, on and on, for hours, through the forest and across the open spaces. For a day at a time he would lie in the underbrush where he could watch the birds and wildlife. But especially he loved to run at midnight, listening to the sleepy murmurs of the forest, and seeking the mysterious "something" that called—called, waking or sleeping, at all times, for him to come.

One night he sprang from sleep with a start, with a scent in his nostrils. From the forest came the call—a long howl. And he knew it, in the old familiar way, as a sound he had heard before. He sprang through the sleeping camp and dashed through the woods.

As he drew closer to the cry he went more slowly, with caution in every movement, till he came to an open place among the trees. Looking out he saw a long, lean timber wolf with his nose pointed to the sky.

Buck had made no noise, yet the wolf stopped howling. Buck stalked into the open, half-crouching, with his tail straight and stiff. He was ready for either an attack or surrender. But the wolf fled at the sight of him. Buck followed, with wild leapings. He ran the wolf into a jammed creek bed, cornering him. The wolf whirled about, snarling and clipping his teeth together.

Buck did not attack, but circled about him in a friendly manner. The wolf was suspicious and afraid. Seeing his chance, the wolf darted away, and the chase was on again. Time and again he was cornered, and then the wolf would escape.

But in the end, the wolf surrendered to Buck's chase and finally sniffed noses with him. Then they became friendly, and romped about like brothers. After some time of this, the wolf started off in a way that plainly showed he was going somewhere. He made it clear to Buck that he was to come. They ran side by side through the early morning hours, straight up the creek bed, and up onto the mountainside.

They came down into a large forest with many streams, and through this wild area they ran on, hour after hour. The sun rose higher and the day grew warmer. Buck was wildly glad. He knew he was at last answering the call, running by the side of his wood brother toward the place where the call came from. Instincts and old memories were stirring within him. He had done this thing before, somewhere in that other world—his dream world. And he was doing it again now, running free in the open with the wide sky overhead.

They stopped by a running stream to drink. Then Buck remembered John Thornton. He sat down. The wolf started on toward the place from where the call surely came, then returned to Buck, sniffing noses. But Buck turned about and started slowly back to camp.

For an hour the wild brother ran by his side, whining softly. Then he sat down, pointed his nose upward, and howled. It was a sad howl, and as Buck trotted back to camp he heard it grow faint and then fainter until it was lost in the distance.

John Thornton was eating dinner when Buck dashed into camp and sprang upon him in a playful romp, licking his face, biting his hand. John Thornton shook Buck back and forth and growled and spoke to him lovingly.

For two days and nights, Buck never left camp and never let Thornton out of his sight. He followed him about at his work, watched him while he ate, saw him into his blankets at night and out of them in the morning. But after two days the call in the forest began to sound more than ever.

Buck thought of his wild brother and of the smiling, wild land that lay outside camp. Once again he took to wandering in the woods, but the wild brother came no more. Buck listened every night. The sad howl was never raised.

# CHAPTER FOURTEEN

# Into the Wilds

Buck began to sleep out at night, staying away from camp for days at a time. Once he crossed the mountain and went down into the land of timber and streams. There he wandered for a week, looking for his wild brother. He fished for salmon and hunted for his food. He killed only to eat. And he was quick, smart, and crafty. No prey was too swift for him—bird, rabbit, or beaver.

By the stream he killed a large black bear that was blinded by the mosquitoes. The bear had raged through the forest with Buck at his heels. It was a hard fight, but Buck took the bear down. He was a master in the wild.

Buck could rely on his own strength and power. His pride showed in the way he carried himself, in every muscle. He looked like a gigantic wolf and he was cunning like a wolf. Yet he had the intelligence of his shepherd mother and St. Bernard father. All this made him one of the fiercest creatures to roam the wild. Every part of him was aware of the sounds and smells and sights around him. He could think faster than any dog and hunt as well as any wild wolf. Even the men noticed that Buck was special.

"Never was there such a dog," said John Thornton one day, as they watched Buck march out of camp.

"When he was made, the mold was broke," said Pete.

"I t'ink so myself," Hans affirmed.

They saw Buck marching out of camp, but they did not see the instant and terrible change that took place as soon as he was within the forest. There he became a thing of the wild, stealing along softly, cat-footed, like a passing shadow.

As the fall of the year came on, the moose herds began to appear. Buck came upon a band of twenty moose one day at the creek. Their chief

was a great bull moose, standing over six feet from the ground. Buck watched the bull moose. Here was a challenge. Back and forth the bull tossed his great antlers. His small eyes glared as he roared with fury at the sight of Buck.

A feathered arrow was sticking out of the bull's side. He was wounded, and Buck took note of this. Buck followed the bull moose and cut him off from the others. Buck barked and danced about in front of the bull, just out of reach of the great antlers and terrible hoofs. The bull was driven into a rage. He charged at Buck, but the crafty dog backed away, toying with the great animal.

Buck was patient. For half a day he kept at the wounded bull. He attacked from all sides, keeping the moose from rejoining the others. The herd tried to help their leader from time to time, but they soon tired of the fierce dog.

As night came, the weary old bull stood with his head lowered. He watched the other moose as they went off in search of food. He could not follow. The fanged dog would not let him go. He was a grand animal and had lived a long, strong life. At the end he faced death at the teeth of another grand animal—a new king.

From then on, night and day, Buck never left the moose. He would not let him eat. He would not let him drink. Buck kept at him, nipping at his legs, waiting for the great bull moose to grow weaker and weaker. At last, at the end of the fourth day, he pulled the great moose down.

For a day and a night he remained by the kill, eating and sleeping. Then he turned his face toward camp and John Thornton.

As he set out on the path for home, he could feel a new stir in the land. He knew—not by sight, or sound, or smell, but by some other sense—that new life was coming into the land. The birds talked of it, the squirrels chattered about it, the very breeze whispered of it. Several times he stopped and drew in the fresh morning air in great sniffs. He read a message which made him leap on with greater speed. He now felt a sense of dread, and as he dropped down into the valley toward camp, he proceeded with greater caution.

Three miles away he came upon a fresh trail that sent his neck hair bristling. It led straight toward camp and John Thornton. Buck hurried on swiftly, with every nerve tense, alert to the details which told a story—all but the end.

He noticed the silence of the forest, as if all life was in hiding.

As Buck slid along like a shadow, his nose picked up a scent that pulled him toward a thicket. There he found Night. He was lying on his side, dead, with a feathered arrow through his body.

From the camp came the faint sound of many voices, rising and falling in a sing-song chant. Bellying forward to the edge of the clearing, he found Hans, lying on his face, feathered with arrows. Then Buck peered out through the trees and saw what made his hair leap straight up on his neck and shoulders. Rage swept over him. He did not know that he growled so loudly. His reason left him and his great love for John Thornton made him react without thinking.

The Yeehats were dancing about the camp's fire when they heard a fearful roaring and saw rushing upon them an animal—a strange and fierce animal they had never seen before. It was Buck, a live hurricane of fury, hurling himself upon them in a frenzy to destroy. He sprang at the closest man, the chief of the Yeehats, grabbing his throat. He did not pause, but leaped

upon a second man. He plunged so quickly that every arrow missed him. In fact, the surprised Indians were so close together and so frantic that they shot one another with the arrows. Then a panic seized the Yeehats, and they fled in terror to the woods, yelling as they fled that the Evil Spirit had come.

And truly Buck was the Evil Spirit raging at their heels and dragging them down like deer as they raced through the trees. It was a fateful day for the Yeehats. They scattered—and it was not till a week later that the last of the survivors gathered together in a lower valley and counted their losses.

Buck, weary of the chase, returned to the empty camp. He found Pete dead in his blankets. Thornton's own struggle was fresh-written on the earth and Buck scented every detail of it down to the edge of a deep pool. By the water's edge lay Skeet, faithful to the end. The pool was muddy and Buck could not see what it contained. But he knew that it contained John Thornton, for Buck followed his trace into the water.

No trace led away.

All day Buck brooded by the pool or roamed about the camp. Buck knew death, and he knew John Thornton was dead. It left him empty. He ached and ached and nothing could fill this emptiness. At times, when he paused at the bodies of the Yeehats, he forgot his pain. He was aware of a great pride in himself. He had killed man and he had killed in the face of the law of club and fang. Never again would he fear this animal.

# CHAPTER FIFTEEN

# Buck Answers the Call

Night came on, and a full moon rose high over the trees into the sky. Buck, lying next to the pool, lifted his head from his mourning and brooding. He stood up, listening and scenting. From far away drifted a faint, sharp yelp, followed by more sharp yelps. He walked to the center of the open space and listened. It was the call—the call of the wild. And now he was ready to follow. John Thornton was dead. The last tie with man was broken.

A wolf pack had crossed over from the land of streams and timber and invaded Buck's valley. Into the clearing they poured, lit by the moonlight.

In the center of the clearing stood Buck, as still as a statue, waiting for them.

They stopped in wonder at this large creature before them. The boldest one leaped straight for him. Like a flash, Buck struck, breaking the neck. Three others tried it, and one after the other they drew back, cut and slashed.

The whole pack then closed in. Buck was too quick and too smart for them. Whirling on his hind legs, and snapping and gashing, he was everywhere at once, leaping from side to side. To prevent the pack from getting behind him, he was forced back down into the creek bed. Here he was finally backed against a high gravel bank. He turned and faced the pack.

For half an hour no wolf could take the cornered beast and the wolves drew back. They remained there. Some were lying down, others were on their feet, watching him. Still others were lapping water from the pool.

One wolf, long and lean and gray, came to Buck slowly, in a friendly manner. Buck recognized his wild brother with whom he had run for a night and a day. He was whining softly, and, as Buck whined, they touched noses.

Then an old battle-scarred wolf came forward. Buck snarled his lips, but sniffed noses with him. The old wolf sat down, pointed nose at the moon, and broke out the long wolf howl. The others sat down and howled. And now the call came to Buck. He, too, sat down and howled.

The pack crowded around him, sniffing. The leaders lifted the call of the pack and sprang away into the woods. The wolves swung in behind, yelping in chorus. And Buck ran with them, side by side with the wild brother, yelping as he ran.

And here may well end the story of Buck.

But it was not many years before the Yeehats noted a change in the breed of timber wolves. Some had splashes of brown on head and muzzle, and a strip of white down the chest. But more remarkable than this, the Yeehats tell of a Ghost Dog that runs at the head of the pack. They are afraid of this Ghost Dog, for it has great cunning—stealing from their camps, robbing their traps, and killing their dogs.

Nay, the tale grows worse. The Indians tell of hunters who never returned to the camp. And they tell of hunters found dead—with wolf prints about them in the snow. These prints were far greater than the prints of any wolf. Each fall, when the Yeehats follow the moose herds, there is a certain valley they never enter. There are women who become sad when the tale is told around the fire of how the Evil Spirit came to live in that valley.

In the summers there is one visitor to that valley, however, that the Yeehats never see. It is a great, beautiful wolf unlike all other wolves. He comes alone from the timber land and walks down into an open space among the trees. Here a golden stream flows into a still pond. He stays by the pond for a time, howling once, long and mournfully, before he departs.

But he is not always alone. When the long winter nights come on, he may be seen running at the head of the pack through the pale moonlight. With a great cry from deep within him he sings a song of the wild, which is the song of the pack.

## THE END

## JACK LONDON

John (Jack) Griffith London was born in 1876 and grew up in San Francisco. He left school at age fourteen and went on to hold many unusual jobs. He was an "oyster pirate," he worked for the Fish Patrol of San Francisco, and he worked on a seal-hunting ship that took him to Japan. He then traveled around the United States. In 1897, he joined the gold rush in the Klondike, in the far north of Alaska and Canada.

In his early twenties, Jack London knew he wanted to be a writer. He was a self-taught man who read and wrote constantly. He continued to travel, sail, and write—about the slums of London, the South Sea islands, boxing, life in the wilds, and life at sea. Some of his more famous works include *The Call of the Wild* (1903), *The Sea-Wolf* (1904), and *White Fang* (1906), which portray scenes and characters from his own experiences.

Jack London had a rich—sometimes wild—life. It was filled with adventure, but it was also filled with illness and private sadness. He died much too early at the age of forty in 1916.